Blessings in Disguise

Blessings in Disguise

Melissa A Regan

Copyright © 2024 Melissa A Regan

All rights reserved.

ISBN: 9798873886302

FOR MY MUM

who has always believed in me and encouraged me to try new things, but never fails to be surprised when I actually do them!

CONTENTS

	Acknowledgments	i
1	Joel's Castle	Pg 13
2	Jane's Race	Pg 19
3	Emily's Orchestra	Pg 25
4	Harry's Assignment	Pg 31
5	David's Handicap	Pg 37
6	Miss Smith's Class	Pg 43
7	Grace's Suntan	Pg 49
8	Ethan's Mortgage	Pg 55
9	Adam's Conducting	Pg 61
10	Brian's Game	Pg 67

ACKNOWLEDGMENTS

Firstly, I must thank my parents, (Jane Wheeler and Christopher Regan) without whom I would not be here literally and figuratively. They have been some of my biggest champions and most constructive critics.

Further gratitude should be offered to their partners Berny and Pat, who have brought a lot of fun and joy to my life. Family holidays and Christmases (with all five of us and my younger brother Peter) have taught me so much about how we can all get along together even in surprising circumstances.

I would also like to acknowledge my Leighton Buzzard parents, Craig and Linda Sheppard, who took me under their wing when I came to a new place on my own. What a beautiful example they have both been to me.

Also, their sons Richard and William. They have both helped me become a better listener, less judgmental and a little bit better at Spanish. Because I knew you, I have been changed for good.

My friends, Amy and Joe Patel, who try to keep me sane and let me play with their adorable children.

Finally, all my friends, family and colleagues. Thank you for supporting me in this journey we call life.

Blessings in Disguise

Blessings in Disguise

Blessings in Disguise

Joel's Castle

If ye then [...] know how to give good gifts unto your children, how much more shall your Father which is in heaven give good things to them that ask him?

- Matthew 7: 11

All Joel wanted was a Lego castle. As it was his birthday soon, he was looking forward to finally getting it. Every time the advert came on, he dragged the closest parent in front of the dazzling TV screen. He could rattle off all the best features: secret passageways, a revolving bookcase, two glass towers and arrow shooting windows. Thinking they might need extra nudging, he covered his parent's room with printed pictures and Amazon prices. Every night, his dreams were filled with the different ways he could construct it or the battles he would enact.

Even though his parents hadn't told him what they were going to get for his birthday, he was sure they would buy him the Lego castle. They had given him more expensive presents before, like the motorised dirt bike, plus he'd been so good the entire year. He had submissively done every arduous chore,

Blessings in Disguise

always offered to wash dishes and even helped his younger sister with her homework. Trembling with anticipation, he couldn't wait until the morning of his birthday when he could unwrap the massive box.

When his birthday dawned, none of the boxes seemed to be the right shape. There were thin ones, which were too long, or round ones that wouldn't have fit enough Lego bricks. There were even soft, pillow-like presents, which he knew couldn't be right. He opened them all, smiling appreciatively at presents from his aunts and uncles, neighbours, parents of friends, and even his favourite chocolate bar, which his sister had saved her precious pocket money to buy him. Dutifully, he made a list of all the thankyou cards he was going to write. Still, where was the present from his parents?

When the floor was strewn with stripy, batman and dragon wrapping paper, his parents led him into the dining room where there was a huge object in the corner, covered by a black, plastic sheet. What could that be? With gentle nudges, Joel's parents encouraged him to go over and see for himself. It did not look like a Lego castle, unless perhaps it had already been built, which would have ruined half the fun.

Blessings in Disguise

Hesitantly, Joel slipped the cover off to reveal a mahogany standing piano. He was very confused. No one in the family played piano. On the stand, was a beginner's book, with a cartoon of a child beaming as he pressed the piano keys. His parents told him they had paid for some lessons as well.

Joel was upset; this was not what he had asked for. What had he done wrong? Wasn't he good enough? Hadn't his requests been sufficiently explicit? Clearly, they had the money to buy the Lego castle, as the piano was much more expensive. They had simply chosen not to listen to him. What was the point in talking to people, who showed no signs of paying attention?

Joel sulked in his bedroom all day and wouldn't even come down for his birthday cake. He told his parents that he did not want to see his friends, choosing to stay in his room and play with Lego train, all the time conscious of how inferior it was compared to the castle.

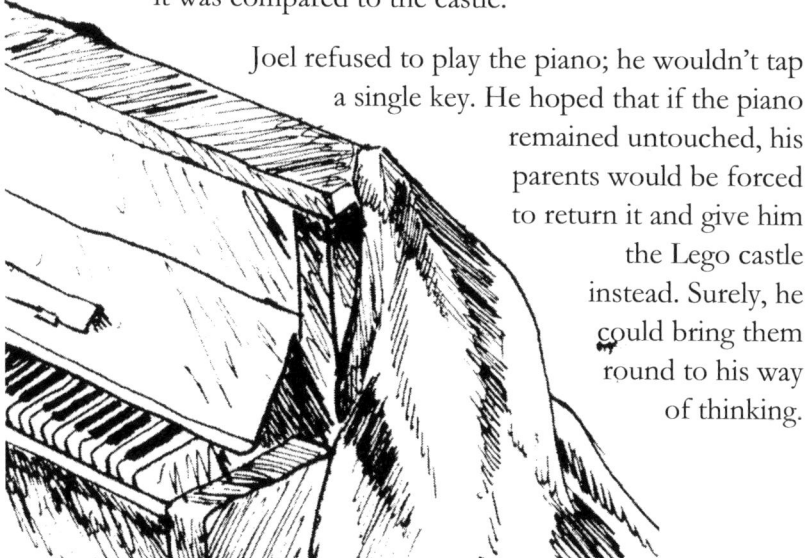

Joel refused to play the piano; he wouldn't tap a single key. He hoped that if the piano remained untouched, his parents would be forced to return it and give him the Lego castle instead. Surely, he could bring them round to his way of thinking.

Blessings in Disguise

A few months later, his little sister started to play about with the neglected piano. She wasn't able to follow the book, but she had fun hearing what different notes sounded like. Joel did not like this at all. He may hate the piano, but it was his piano and the only present his parents had given him that year. So, one day, before anyone else had woken up, Joel' snuck down and tentatively pressed some of the keys. By the time his parents appeared to make breakfast, he'd worked out how to play Twinkle Twinkle little star by himself.

Joel took the lessons, delighting in playing different pieces of music. He got on well with his teacher and progressed fast. In record time, he had passed his grade one with a distinction. Joel was really proud of himself. As soon as he got his results, he threw himself in to trying to work out the grade two pieces.

Later that week, as he practised some of the new scales, his parents sidled into the room. They carried a big bag between them, which was the size and shape that Joel had once dreamt about. When they said it was for him, he was surprised. Joel opened it and found the Lego castle he had always wanted. Immediately, he took it upstairs and began constructing it.

Joel spent two weeks building the Lego castle, which only took so long because he spent hours on the piano as well. Every afternoon for a week, he played with the fully constructed version and at the weekend, his friends came over to use to its full capacity. They had great fun.

By his next birthday, Joel had stopped playing with the Lego castle and it sat in the corner of his room, hoping he might play with it the next Christmas. However, his life was filled with grades, concerts and compositions. Nothing brought him more joy than his own family gathering around the mahogany piano while he played.

As he grew up their faces changed but the warm feeling never dimmed. While the Lego castle was eventually given away, Joel used his piano throughout his life.

Blessings in Disguise

Jane's Race

I have fought a good fight, I have finished my course, I have kept the faith:

- *2 Timothy 4:7*

This was the morning that Jane would run her duathlon. It was as warm as could be expected in England and the air held a beautiful fragrance of promise. All summer, she'd been bubbling with excitement about completing the race; now was the moment to relish. Although she knew that she wasn't the faster runner, she felt good about her cycling abilities. It was something she wanted to do and she was determined to enjoy it.

Going with her mother to sign up had made her a little nervous. Pinning the bold number '21' on her back made it very official. Decided. There was no turning back now. Also, it was the first opportunity to meet her competition. There were taller, leaner children, those with more developed muscles. They had sparkly new bikes in racing red, electric blue or winning gold. Most of them were also older than her, benefitting from more practice and probably having planned a better strategy. Some of them were even confident enough to come without their parents, happy to ask a stranger to help them pin on their number. Suddenly, Jane felt very out of place and completely overwhelmed.

By the time everyone was instructed to gather at the starting line, Jane was reluctant to join them. There were just so many spectators. The grass track was surrounded by hoards of parents and friends, every eye on the participants. Jane was scared of what they would all think of her, frightened of their laughter if she fell behind. The course, which had seemed so exciting when other people were competing, was suddenly a horrible place where she would be separated from her family.

Gathering the children close, the announcer described the course. The first section was a short run around half of the track before they picked up their bikes. This seemed an easy way to get the children used to the race. Then there was the dangerous changing station where it was more than likely people would crash into one another. This could easily result in them toppling over like dominos as they tried to get used to their bikes when several of them had barely been off training wheels. That was one of the make-or-break moments, where the choices about steering and speed were vitally important. This would probably determine their positions for the majority of the cycling, unless they were particularly skilled at overtaking on narrow paths.

They were then expected to ride around the outside of the arena, hidden from most of the crowd by a row of trees. This was a disappointingly short stretch, not even half the length of all the running. Jane chewed her lip at the news. Finally, there was another run, which went far out from the main track. They would be completely alone for most of this, until they arrived back in the circle under the eyes of the crowd.

It was what it was; there was no changing it and there was no way to avoid the obstacles that were bound to appear. Jane lined up with the others, content with the second row, rather than jostling her way into the front. She tried to prepare herself: breathe naturally, grip the earth with her flimsy trainers and hold her hands flat like she had been taught. However, none of it mattered because when the starting gun fired there was only blind panic.

Most of the children set off at a terrific pace; Jane could almost see the dust clouds they kicked up. For a moment she thought of copying them, but she knew she could only maintain a slower stride. During the first run she hovered at the back of the group, steadily overtaking those that had overestimated their sprinting ability. Although some of the young boys were furious to slip behind her, short bursts were unsustainable.

By the time she got to her bike she had a reasonable position. Her mother was waiting with her bike upright, ready for Jane to hop on. They managed the switch well and Jane was soon pedalling out of the changing station. She noticed that several of the other children had been pushed along by their parents for quite a distance, whereas Jane had been immediately deserted. Whilst she thought it was unfair of her mother not to give as much help as possible, she didn't let the worry interfere with her riding.

Feet spinning, Jane managed to sneak up a couple of places. She kept riding to the very edge of the second changing station, dropping her bike without a thought. After being off the bike, her legs felt very wobbly, making the run even more difficult. Whilst this affected all of the competitors, Jane seemed to suffer more. She just kept going, even though people were already rushing past her.

As the group ran further away from the original track, Jane began to feel increasingly tired. She couldn't help but feel disappointed by the amount of people overtaking her. With tears starting to cloud her vision she stumbled along the grass. As Jane stepped onto the uneven surface of the path that led back to the track, her knee buckled and she fell among the hard stones.

She had fallen awkwardly, one leg folded beneath her and the knee had a massive gouge out of it. As the last two people behind her came puffing past, Jane discovered blood coming from the wound. Already weakened, she doubted whether she even had the strength to stand up again. It was pointless, the time she had spent on the floor added to the hobble she would endure to finish meant that she would be embarrassingly slow. They may even have begun the race for the older children before she made it back. The hopelessness of the situation caused tears to mingle with the blood on her hands.

To Jane it felt like forever, but soon her mother was at her side encouraging her to get up. This only made Jane cry harder and protest that it was too much to expect of her. She just wished that her mother would scoop her up in her arms and carry her to wherever the rest of the family were. No one else's parent would have been so anxious to force their child through more pain. Jane really felt like the unluckiest girl in the world.

Her mother did not lift her up, she did not stop urging her to finish the race and she did not go away. Instead she kept expressing how disappointed Jane would be with herself if she did not complete the course. Jane could not agree with this, the nominal crossing of the line seemed thoroughly pointless from this position. It would only involve a lot of effort and even more embarrassment. She pleaded for her mother to hoist her onto her shoulders and cross the line together. She was told that this would not be fair on the other participants and that she would not get the same warm feeling inside.

It was agony. Every step Jane took she thought her left leg would buckle again because her bleeding knee hurt so much. Would the wound ever heal? Perhaps her soft skin marred by an ugly scar, which made Jane feel even more like giving up. She was upset that her mother did not seem to be taking the situation seriously enough. So, she cried as she hobbled along. This did nothing to outwardly increase her mother's sympathy with the situation. She simply walked alongside her daughter, ceaselessly encouraging her to endure to the end.

The path opened up into the main track. Jane could see the finish line, but the course swerved around the longer semi-circle of the track. She wanted to take the short cut, but one look from her mother removed any possibility of that. Still feeling unbelievably hard done by, Jane started to walk more normally, even attempting a loping jog as some of the spectators caught sight of her.

With her mother still at her side, Jane continued to the growing sound of applause. She had never seen so many smiling faces and they were all directed at her. There were complete strangers clapping their hands together and urging her to take those final steps across the line. She spotted her father and brother near the end, eager for her to join them on the other side of the line. They were waving their hands, furiously beckoning her on, unable to physically help her, but she finally felt the emotional support she had needed the most.

She couldn't quite remember how she had crossed the line. Her mother said that she collapsed in the grass on the other side. She had memories of a golden medal with triumphant runners engraved on it being thrust into her hands. There was a blur of people grinning at her, helping her stand, walking with her to join the lucky spectators. Ice-cream materialised with a chunky flake wedged in the delicious cone. She sat down and smiled. She rubbed her fingers against the runners on the medal and fingered the red-white-and-blue striped ribbon.

For the rest of the day people congratulated her, recognising her above any other participants. It didn't matter that she had been the last to cross the line; everyone was just proud that she had finished at all. The winners had run a good race, but with the help of a persistent mother, Jane had overcome the most.

Emily's Orchestra

For unto every one that hath shall be given, and he shall have abundance: but from him that hath not shall be taken away even that which he hath.

- Matthew 25:29

Emily and James had been having violin lessons with Mrs Williams for seven years. Every week, Emily would go to Mrs Williams' house straight after school for half an hour before her mum picked her up. James, who was in the year above, turned up on his BMX for the slot after hers. Over time, they had gotten to know one another, especially as Mrs Williams exhibited a frightening habit of making them perform together. Emily's caution and steady practice balanced James's natural ability and confidence, so that they were of a similar standard.

One September, Mrs Williams proposed they both joined the community orchestra that met in Headingtree town hall. Emily was anxious about the idea because there were so many adults whom she had heard playing well. However, her mother reassured her that fourteen was quite old enough and promised to drive her to the town hall after dinner each Wednesday evening. With trepidation, Emily agreed.

Blessings in Disguise

The columns of the town hall loomed over Emily, imposing their four and a half centuries of age upon her young mind. Her mother waved from the car: in an instant she was gone. Suddenly, the fraying bottle-green violin case weighed heavily in Emily's trembling hand. A man with silver hair neatly combed back strode into the building carrying a small flute case. When he held the door open, Emily had no other option but to follow him inside.

The chairs were already set up; tubas, trumpets and horns were blasting noises like a heard of elephants whilst the conductor leafed through the music on her stand. Emily couldn't see James anywhere and hoped that she would not be deserted for long. Without catching any eyes, she found a spot in the corner and unzipped her case. Her shoulder rest fitted, her bow rosined and tightened, she joined an awkward group of violin players hanging behind the two rows of paired seats. They glanced warily at the regular players, who had already sat down. Emily counted a few pairs in the middle and one person sat confidently at the front.

"Do you play first or second?" A lanky man asked the group of new comers. A couple near Emily immediately answered and were shown to a pair of seats.

Emily wished Mrs Williams had thought to explain these terms before sending her on this fearful mission. Filled with a sense of her own stupidity and lack of belonging, she squeaked "Which is the easiest?" when the stick insect turned to her.

A warm smile spread across the man's face and he suggested that she joined the seconds. Once more, Emily looked about her to see whether James had magically appeared. She was just about to slide into the spare seat in the back row, when the conductor motioned her to come to the front. For a moment Emily froze. Was it really to her that she was madly flapping? How could she possibly be asked to sit that far forward where everyone would expect her to be so good? They hadn't even heard her play. Somehow, it must have all been Mrs Williams' doing. Still, Emily was too frightened to ignore or disobey the conductor's persistent waving and traipsed towards the front desk.

Before Emily could even settle into her new position, the baton was raised and the piece began. Her partner had not introduced himself so she followed his cue, hoping that someone would use his name before she had to or resort to addressing him as 'sir'. They were playing Myzortky's 'Pictures at an Exhibition', the title and composer being the only things on the page that Emily could understand. Besides the notes being too high, fast and unpredictable, there were several markings that Emily could only suppose were reserved for the orchestra elite. When there were two notes to be played at the same time Emily wasn't sure whether she was allowed to share

them between her silent desk partner or attempt a wild cross string motion that she had only witnessed Mrs Williams demonstrate a couple of times. However, she was usually too lost and flummoxed to play either.

It was two hours from a special circle of Hell. Half-way through all the violins whispered 'mutes' to each other, like a secret code. They then proceeded to produce small plastic semi-circles that rested on their strings. Emily had never seen one before, and adjusted by playing even quieter. Then there had been the moment when she finally felt confident about the 'd' and played a beat before anyone else. How mortifying! By the end of the rehearsal, Emily couldn't believe that the conductor had let her remain in the front. It must have been some tortuous initiation for new comers. She only just had enough resolve to prove to them and herself that she wasn't quite that bad.

As everyone got up to leave, Emily caught sight of James, who must have sidled in part way through without her noticing. He was leant back in his chair, like a sunbather in their hammock, listening to the man lounged beside him chatting amicably. Seeing Emily's exhausted expression, he chuckled in such a low tone that only she could notice. Evidently, it was much more fun and less pressure at the back. Whilst she envied his position, she did not dare display any more weakness than had already been demonstrated.

The weeks of that first term before Christmas followed a similar pattern. Emily felt that everyone judged her numerous early, late, flat or completely unexpected notes and James merely relaxed in the back. He was enjoying himself far more than she was, especially as he was wholly invisible to the conductor. Yet she had been called by name without Emily ever having even given it to the conductor. Her ears must have burnt and her cheeks flushed for every second of it. The two hours always seemed the longest and most excruciating of the week, but she persevered. She didn't always know why or feel sure that it would ever be worth it, but something stopped her from leaving.

A glimmer of change twinkled at the first concert in December. Emily was accustomed to the piece now, knew some fingering to make the sections easier, was aware of which notes she could get away with emphasising and had divided all of the double notes with her desk partner. Nothing went perfectly, but it was over much quicker than Emily had expected. As she stood up at the end a unique feeling of elation washed over her. She has been a part, however small, of something great and her contribution was applauded rather than rejected. Standing at the front of the semi-circle she could see each of the faces clapping her and the conductor smiled at her as she shook the leader's hand.

The concert increased Emily's confidence during the second term. The fast sections no longer filled her with such overwhelming anxiety, because she knew eventually she would be able to muddle through them. Little by little, she started speaking to Ben her desk partner about his family. It even became apparent that he was not as perfect at counting as she had previously presumed. Each Wednesday, she leapt up from dinner, rather than dragging her heels and she wasn't as exhausted each time she returned home.

However, she could not help but notice that James's attendance became more haphazard. What had been relaxing before, became boring. One week, as they crossed paths for Mrs Williams' lessons, Emily caught him bringing his bike around the back.

"I don't see you so much at orchestra now," she stated.

"Yeah, well, you don't have to go *every* week," he responded.

"I know," Emily admitted, biting her lip, "but it makes it easier if you do. I feel like Ben is teaching me loads!"

"No one in the back rows comes all the time, we're not like you swots up the front."

Before he could say anymore, Emily hurried off home, mulling over the benefits of her hard-working group in comparison to James' surroundings of half-hearted players.

By the time April bloomed, they were due to perform their Easter concert and James was not allowed to play because he had missed too many rehearsals. He brushed it off, saying he didn't want to be part of it anyway. Still, he didn't look pleased when his Mum forced him to come and watch Emily from the audience. Whilst James began to bury his talent and had failed to reach his potential, Emily was blessed twice over for her commitment and dedication through difficult circumstances.

Harry's Assignment

Come unto me, all ye that labour and are heavy laden and I will give you rest. Take my yoke upon you, and learn of me; for I am meek and lowly in heart: and ye shall find rest unto your souls. For my yoke is easy, and my burden is light.

- *Matthew 11:28-30*

Harry needed to get a 2:1 in his degree in order to earn his place on the internship in Canary Wharf. Whilst he allowed himself time to be spent stand-up watching, karaoke-singing, midnight-munching and film-watching with his friends, academic success was his primary concern. Even when taking breaks back home in Cumbria, he always heaved textbooks in his rucksack to be studied on the train. It was one of the few opportunities where he could remove himself from the rest of the world and focus. He felt he was learning the most, curled up in the corner seat, closer to the landscape rushing by than the other passengers.

However, good results had never come easily to Harry. His lack of natural talent and undisruptive behaviour meant that he had been overlooked in school. When he announced his acceptance into Royal Holloway University, people were neither surprised nor held high expectations of him. His parents simply packed their car with an Asda price iron, clothes' horse, plastic cutlery, Dell laptop and Harry's clothes.

Then, they proceeded to drive him down to the campus and left him to his own devices, trusting him to continue in mediocrity.

The first year had gone remarkably well. Harry diligently applied himself to each task within the confines of his prison-walled bedroom. The course guide was self-explanatory and Harry believed he had remembered everything of importance after a couple of reads. He saw  no need to use his seminar leaders' office hours because he was achieving a high 2:1 across all his modules by himself. Besides, their available hours often conflicted with Rugby practice or eating lunch with his friends. If they really wanted to talk to him, he was sure that they would take the initiative and email him. It was common practice to only interact with them during seminars and work any problems out in his own time.

The change came in second year. Harry had found a good house only fifteen minutes' walk from the university, so he saw no reason for his grades to drop. He did not spend any more time with his friends than he had done the first year. In fact, he found himself spending most of his time in the library, reading more widely than before and scribbling as many notes as he could. However, after his second-year exams he had 55% - not the 2:1 he needed for the internship.

Harry was shocked. How had this happened? Surely, the adjustment between school and university had been made; the difference between the years should have been minimal. To worsen matters, his first-year grade wouldn't even count towards his final mark. Whilst everyone was celebrating their success, or lamenting missing out on a first, Harry shared his results with hardly anyone. He hoped that he could be passed over and his results forgotten. He worked at Barracudas summer camp and soon found himself in the September of his final year.

He had never felt so despondent in his life. What had been the point of all those books read, all those extra hours revising? The university system did not seem to be a fair representation of a student's ability. It took all of Harry's efforts to drag himself out of bed in the morning and made the head-phoned walk to his lecture. He took notes, but doubted that they would be useful because he didn't know what he was meant to be listening for anymore. There was so much information squashed into each hour and every lecturer differed so much in what they deemed important that Harry felt completely overwhelmed.

Half-way through October, Harry's course was set the obligatory mid-term assignment. He went through the usual steps of reading the compulsory list of chapters and articles, choosing the ones he felt were most relevant for detailed study. Then, he watched a series of documentaries on the subject that interested him. Finally, he wrote a first draft of the 2,000 words, leaving a week to edit it while he completed the reading for the next lecture.

Peter was a friend of a friend that had moved into their house that year after a previous housemate had graduated. He was taking the same modules as Harry and doing better. Harry had heard Peter praised by several seminar leaders as innovative, which made him feel intimidated by the new housemate's presence. His zealous and ultimately fruitless effort was sure to be discovered and mocked. However, when Harry had completed his first draft, Peter asked him to help cut some words out of his own assignment so that it would fit the word count. Harry was curious about Peter's magic formula and agreed.

Reading Peter's essay made Harry panic more. He made some uncertain suggestions, stressing his own incompetence. Peter thanked him and emailed their seminar leader to get some more advice. Harry was now so confused as to the nature of their assignment that he decided to arrange to meet with their seminar leader.

The next morning, Harry stood outside Dr Richardson's door, still not expecting to make any major changes to his essay. He imagined that Dr Richardson might just correct some of his imperfect grammar and propose a little restructuring that would suddenly transform the assignment from 55% to 75%. He planned what to say and any questions that he could think of before knocking on the oak door.

Those 20 minutes of discussion gave Harry a better insight to Dr Richardson and her expectations than he had gleaned from the entire three years. The conversation flowed more freely that he had expected. To begin, Dr Richardson looked over the entire essay and listened attentively to what Harry had to say. Harry had not foreseen her caring enough to read the whole thing; he had always believed that seminar leaders simply read the introduction and conclusion to make an impulsive decision. Yet his experience disproved any of his earlier hypotheses.

Once Harry had run out of ways to phrase his concern, Dr Richardson stared back at him, her ballpoint pen poised over the last sentence she had underlined. In that moment, she measured the situation and the character of her student.

"You can get a 2:1 on this essay," she pronounced.
"But not in its current state?" Harry checked.
"No."
"Can you give me enough help to make it a first; I need to pull up my grade from last year?" Harry's fingers were already reaching for the paper, his eyes searching to see what adjustments he would have to make.

"I can't promise that," Dr Richardson smiled, "Are you willing to completely submit to my judgements and not temper my decades of experience with your own opinion?"

"Of course," Harry replied, conscious that any other answer was both insulting and detrimental to his own progress.

"Are you also prepared to leave this office and do everything as though it all depended on you, rather than trying to shift the blame onto my marking?"

Harry nodded. Dr Richardson passed back the essay and drew her student's attention to the problematic areas. Instead of giving him simple solutions she looked to Harry to think of the possibilities. They discussed each one, Harry conscious that he was being encouraged to speak the most. Once Dr Richardson deemed him to have put in enough of his own effort, she suggested a couple of books in the library that would help ground his essay in more relevant evidence than he had used. Harry scrawled their titles at the bottom of the page, realising that they came from a section of the library he was yet to discover.

Harry left Dr Richardson's office feeling much better. He didn't understand why he had ignored this personal relationship with seminar leaders before. Dr Richardson had been genuinely glad to see Harry and had given him some much-needed direction. When Harry received a 72% for his interim assignment, he confidently attributed it to his call on Dr Richardson's time and never failed to talk to his seminar leader about his concerns again.

Blessings in Disguise

David's Handicap

Let us run with patience the race that is set before us

- *Hebrews 12:1*

David was determined to win. He assessed the neatly mown grass. Rustling in the breeze was the red and white striped spectator tape. In the centre of the track, was the winner's podium, glistening in the rising sun. Dazzling and polished, the medals awaited their victors. Breathing deeply, he could smell the still-wet paint from marking the outline of the oval 300m metre track. The wooden pegs were just as fresh; some of the initials only added minutes before.

The wooden pegs were essential items in the upcoming bicycle race. Bearing their names in scarlet paint, each one was assigned a competitor. They were then placed at different points around the track to mark from where each cyclist should start. The entire year, the race organisers had been watching, recording and monitoring the participants' performance. The fastest were placed at the back so that they would have to ride nearly a whole lap further, while the slowest merited a place near the front. Each had been positioned according to their ability as judged by wise and experienced organisers, who had directed similar events.

Ducking beneath the tape with his bike, David headed to where he believed he would find his marker. The one he had noticed did not bear his initials so he wandered around the vicinity in hopes of locating it. When he could not find it, he went towards the slowest riders because he believed that most of the people present were better than him. This proved just as fruitless. Now, the majority of the riders had taken their positions and were mounting their bikes. A couple of David's friends were near the front, one was eyeing up the competition and the other enjoying the first rays of sun. David was just about to persuade one of them to share their spot with him, when he noticed his wife waving wildly and pointing at a stick in the grass.

David could hardly believe his eyes! It was not the furthest back, but there would be few people behind him. He would have an impossible task just to catch-up with and finish in the bunch. Why did his friends have it so easy and yet the organisers had made it so difficult for him? There was no way that this could be fair. What had David done to offend the organisers? There must be some reason for the injustice. Any hope that David had entertained that he could win this race had evaporated.

His wife continued to usher him over and smile encouragingly. As he crossed the centre of the track, the commentator caught his eye to hurry him up. Everyone, except David, was bristling to start. He planted his bike by the marker, not daring to inch it forward with everyone watching him. Tiredly, he swung his leg over the frame and heaved himself into the saddle. He could hear the squeak of clenched handlebars and the click of toe grips on pedals. He copied, but didn't bother to lean low over the bike; aerodynamics would not be enough to save him. Noticing his despondency, his wife rubbed his back and whispered, "There's no point giving up before you've even tried. You know the organisers; they are just and fair. They want as many people to cross the line together as possible."

As the gun was shot, David determined to do his best. Perhaps he would be able to just catch the rider in front of him; it was worth a try. The man in front, who was called Tony, had been enjoying the prime of his cycling career as he was a little younger than David. He had won several of the races that year, usually staying close behind the faster riders to be protected from the wind and then slipping ahead of them at the end. He had a reputation for being a tactical rider and David usually stayed clear of him.

David found he was gaining ground on Tony remarkably quickly. He was able to hold his bike reasonably steady, which helped propel him forward. Still, he was surprised to be making such easy work of it. He also noticed that the girl (Alison) in front of them had kept further ahead of Tony than David had expected. When David was side by side with Tony, he could see that he wasn't pedalling as fast as he could and that there was no look of concentration on his face. As David passed him, he worried that Tony would try and stay on his wheel and ride off his effort. However, David found himself getting a better lead on Tony as they completed the first lap.

Alison was catching the bunch that was forming, but David began to believe that he could at least draw level with her by the end. He dared to look over his shoulder and discovered that Samuel at the back had already given up and decided to steer into the middle of the track, forfeiting the race. He didn't seem to have experienced any mechanical problems. Evidently, he had not made the progress he wanted and didn't want to stay the distance. David felt disappointed that an admired rider had given up so easily. Now the pressure was on not to let the side down. He couldn't let the people at the front, who had it comparatively easy, monopolise the race. Clenching his jaw, he pushed on.

When David reached the third and final lap, he was metres behind Alison. She was riding strong. She hadn't looked to either side once during the race, benefitting from a level of focus that didn't allow her to compare herself with others. David found himself following her to overtake a very young rider, Ben. He had been positioned at the front, started with exceptional speed, but was unable to maintain it. David gave a sympathetic smile at Ben as he passed, wishing he could have been more consistent.

As they rounded into the straight, David pulled out to draw level with the line of riders that was forming. He could hear the screams of encouragement from his family. Even his seven-year-old daughter called out that Tony wouldn't make it. Looking across the bend of the track, David saw Tony furiously pedalling in desperation. His legs were spinning, beads of sweat dripping from his forehead and steam seemingly coming from his back tire. However, it was too little; too late.

David could feel the wind rushing past as the participants battled for the finish. His two friends were on the inside, contending with one another and oblivious to David's remarkable feat. If they had noticed his presence, they were not surprised or jealous that he had ridden faster than them. There was an older man, with tufts of white hair sticking out of his helmet, that had held his ground and was just being engulfed by the finishing group. It seemed as though the track had stretched to an infinite width, so that everyone crossed the line at a similar time and no one was sure who had technically won.

They had all been so close that it didn't matter. Apart from Samuel, who had given up; Tony, who had left it too late and Ben, who had not been able to maintain his pace. Anyone else could have been crowned the winner because they had fulfilled their potential. They may have ridden different distances, but due to the organisers' handicapping, their effort and success had been equal.

Blessings in Disguise

Miss Smith's Class

Who shall separate us from the love of Christ? shall tribulation, or distress, or persecution, or famine, or nakedness, or peril, or sword? […] Nay, in all these things we are more than conquerors through him that loved us.
- *Romans 8:35, 37*

Miss Smith was acclaimed to have the best classroom in the school. The walls were adorned with the children's work: imaginative stories, mosaiced patterns, geometric designs and carboard maps. Each of these was carefully chosen to showcase a range of skills and lovingly double mounted on sugar paper. Beside each of the stories was a photograph of its author who, when an IPad was raised to it, magically came to life and spoke the adventure aloud. The ceilings were festooned with tricky words to spell and phonics sounds that twirled around in their star-shaped cut-outs. Every bookshelf was fully stacked, every table neatly arranged, every desk clear of clutter and every surface sparkling clean.

After Miss Smith amended the date on her whiteboard, she looked around and saw that it was good. All the handouts had been neatly placed on the centre of each table. Pairs of scissors were laid by each seat alongside a glue stick for the matching activity the pupils would soon be doing. She had given directions for the teaching assistant about how to support certain children during this particular lesson. She took a deep breath; it was ready.

Children smiled as they came in, felt free to hug their parents goodbye, take their time to find their allotted seat and get straight on with their task. There was a happy chatter that allowed comfort, while maintaining respect. Coats were hung up and bags tucked beneath the cloakroom benches. Kitty found a pencil that had slipped out of Ellie's bag and immediately returned it. Grace proudly carried the office correspondence to Miss Smith. Most were already in their seats about the business of learning.

Miss Smith had only to stand at the front of the class with her arms folded and silence reigned. Every eye was on her, waiting for feedback on their first task. She took answers from several of the children, one from each table of six. She listened to each, repeated it back in a manner generally considered easier to understand or closer to the truth and then praised the contribution.

This lesson was not dissimilar to many other lessons she had facilitated. Maths was always first on a Monday and this particular Monday the class would be tackling word problems. Due to the nature of language, no matter how simple the mathematical calculation contained within, word problems always pose a special challenge for children. There is a certain difficulty in perceiving the numbers between the lines and sniffing out the correct operation. This was no different in Miss Smith's class. When the learning objective was revealed, there was a disgruntled sign even her pupils could not disguise.

The concept was modelled; the children involved. Miss Smith had to talk them through reading, understanding, calculating and answering the question. Another example was presented to the class with easier numbers and more transparent language so that one of the higher achieving children was able to explain it to the others. Miss Smith was still sceptical, but she knew that she had to let them work it out for themselves eventually. She could demonstrate all the knowledge in the world theoretically on her pure white board, but it would mean little to them until they experienced it for themselves. It would be through working independently that they would have the opportunity to learn and prove what they could do.

So, she sent them off to their tables to sit with other children of a similar mathematical ability. With those that struggled the most, including those that had yet to master their number bonds to ten, she sent her teaching assistant to help guide them. She knew that without the extra support, they would not even be able to attempt the simpler questions. They would have quickly grown bored and fallen into disruptive activities. The groups above them had the same word problems, but were being encouraged to work more independently. She would ensure that she cheered them on regularly in case there had been an error in her judgement. The middle table were eager to please and try new things by themselves. They had a more difficult sheet and would need reminding to check their work and correct any answers they had mismatched owing to their hastiness.

The top table felt somewhat removed from the rest of the class. Last year, they had not been stretched enough, the work they had been given was easy for them and so they had become complacent. Also, there had been an extra adult in that room because the school had taken trainee teachers into that class and they had grown used to individual attention. In their cleverness, they had realised that they could get far more answers right far quicker if they relied on the knowledge of the trainee who sat with them and were happy to take full advantage of that. Now, it was time to challenge them.

The room hummed with clipping scissors, shuffling papers, smearing glue and whispered discussion. As predicted, few were getting on very well. The teaching assistant had taken to working through one question at a time with the whole table. Near the front, pupils were merely cutting every question and every answer, procrastinating the time they would have to think about what the problems were actually asking of them. Miss Smith moved around the class, watching the children work and pointing out mistakes they had overlooked. The queries and misconceptions on the middle tables kept her so busy that she never wandered over to the top table near the window. Whenever she did look in that direction, they had their heads down.

The minutes ran away as they always did and slowly the children made progress. Miss Smith had to stop less, only hovering over shoulders rather than pointing at the important words and phrases. Just as she was considering stopping the class, she saw Obi's hand go up from the top table. Immediately, she went towards him.

"Miss, Miss!" he called as she came within earshot, "I still don't understand this one, Miss."

"Let's see if we can help," Miss Smith smiled, crouching down so that she was at Obi's level. She looked at his book, the questions and answers neatly cut and placed next to one another. He had not attempted as many problems as she would have expected in the time and only half were correct. "What clues can we find for what the operation might be?"

"I don't know," Obi replied glumly, "It's not like the first one because it doesn't say 'altogether'."

"Yes, well," Miss Smith searched for the best way to help Obi discover the answer for himself, "'Altogether' is not the only word that could mean it's an addition calculation. Do you remember any of the others we talked about last week?" When she was met with silence, she looked around for a prompt, "what about the terms over there on the Maths display by table 5?"

Obi looked blankly at the words so far away that it would require him to move in order to read them. "Miss, why don't you care about us?"

Miss Smith was caught off guard. Hoping Obi would not notice the tear glisten in her eyes, she swallowed the lump that came to her throat. "What do you mean, not care about you? I'm interested in all my pupils."

"Well, why do you care about them more?" Obi moaned, nodding his head towards table five clustered around the teaching assistant.

"I think of you all equally."

"But you don't *treat* us equally. You always put Mrs Hill with one of the other tables or you give them really easy work or you put all the words and numbers near them. I would get much better scores if you treated me like them."

Miss Smith pressed her lips into a smile. "Giving you all the same things isn't treating you equally. Everybody needs different resources to flourish. I would be holding you back if I put you in the same situation as table five. You're a lot better than you think right now, and you need a chance to prove it. Not to me, I already have a pretty good idea, but to yourself."

Obi still didn't finish all the problems that lesson, because his mind was reflecting on something more important. If he was working hard, that meant it was probably worth it. While he would often still feel the sting of hard work and the loneliness of the table, he tried to remember that his teacher did care about all of them, even if she showed it differently to each individual.

Grace's Suntan

In your patience possess ye your souls.
    - *Luke 21:19*

Grace had been waiting for this holiday in the Canary Islands all year. The white sand beaches, the emerald palm trees and glorious sunshine were calling her name. While she still enjoyed a good waterpark, she had reached the age when sunbathing was equally attractive to the adrenaline rush and so she was dying to escape to the warm weather. As soon as her family had wheeled their suitcases into the white washed walls and slippery tiled floors of their hotel, Grace was spinning around ready to go straight to the deck chairs by the pool.

"Aren't you forgetting something?" her mother called with an attempt at a breezy tone.

"I told you Mum, I can read books on my phone," Grace replied, almost out the door already.

"Just wait a moment," came the counter and then an uneasy silence while her mother rummaged through the plastic bag in which she had transported all her liquids past security. The travel sized shampoo went flying across the shining floor; the hand-sized deodorant can clanged against it and other items skittered by. Finally, she pulled out the tube she had been looking for, "here it is."

"Oh Mum, I don't need that," Grace dismissed with

Blessings in Disguise

the flick of her hand.

She could feel her mother's eyes surveying every inch of her opalescent skin. The only thing to darken the ivory colour were numerous little freckles not only across her face, but scattering every limb of her body. "Don't give me any of that nonsense!" was the retort and the bright blue and orange tube was thrust into her hands.

Grace thought she was doing her mother a favour by at least looking at the label. "Factor 50!" she shrieked, "Come on, you need to give my skin some chance at bronzing a little!"

However, all her arguments were in vain as her mother insisted on smothering her in a thick, creamy layer of sun cream before she was able to slip out of the room.

The surface of the pool shimmered like a million tiny fairy lights as Grace strode through the lines of loungers. Each beam could reach the very heart of you and warm the soul as well as the body. Swinging the striped umbrella to one side so that she had optimal view of the sun, Grace stretched each leg carefully out along the bleached white plastic. She did the same with her arms, turning the pasty inside skin towards the uninterrupted azure sky. Nestling her head into the cushioned rest, she prepared to soak up every last ray.

There were already several other sunbathers in the area. Grace tried just to relax and keep her eyes closed, but she couldn't resist watching everyone from beneath the protection of her sunglasses. At the end of her row there was a young woman in a polka dot bikini, who had the most perfect shade of olive skin Grace had ever seen. Such skin wasn't usually trapped in dreary England- that was for sure. Then a pair of boys wriggled out of the pool and they too were blessed with wonderfully tanned skin. Even the old man with a fair-sized belly, thin wisps of white hair and more wrinkles than veins had well bronzed skin. Grace removed the glasses for a moment to check that the tint hadn't been deceiving her yet she truly was just surrounded by enviously sun kissed skin.

Sighing to herself, she flopped back against the chair, woefully aware of the sun cream which blocked the sun from her.

The next two days passed in a similar manner. Whether the family were lazing on the beach, gawking at the cultural sights, dining al fresco or scouring souvenir shops, Grace was not permitted to leave the hotel room without a thick layer of sun cream. This was then reapplied several times throughout the day despite the arguments. Every evening she would stare at her arms, wondering whether she could change their colour by sheer willpower, but they remained as pearly white as the moment they arrived.

On the third day, Grace could stand it no longer. Rather than protesting the need for sun cream, she asked her mother where it was and slipped into the bathroom. Merely pretending to apply it, she reappeared and announced that she was going to explore the rock pools a few minutes' walk from the hotel. She even waved the blue and orange bottle under her mother's nose as she exited the building, listing the times it would be best to reapply it that day.

Finally, she was free from the suffocating clutches of her parents. She could make her own choices and give her skin the chance to turn a more appealing shade. All morning, she enjoyed climbing about the various rock formations in her swimming costume. She could feel the sun tickling her back like a good friend who had not been seen in a long time. While she paddled her feet in the mirror-like water, she turned her face up to the sky and gloried in this chance to be alive. After she had tired of clambering from one point to another, Grace found a sandy spot and lay down in the soporific sun. Within minutes she had drifted off into a relaxed snooze that would last much of the afternoon.

Grace woke to a mild itching sensation, as though mice were scurrying up and down her arms. Batting her eyelids open, she stretched her mouth into a yawn. The action made her skin feel more taut than usual, like it was covered in a layer of clingfilm. Before she got up from her recumbent position, Grace noticed how pink the skin of her thighs looked. The way the sun hung low on the horizon suggested how long she may have been snoozing.

All of the things she had observed and felt in those first moments of consciousness, increased over the rest of the evening. She tried to dismiss her mother's numerous 'I told you so' speeches, but this became ever more difficult to ignore as the pink hue of her skin turned more and more crimson. By the time she lay down to sleep, the skin on her legs were in agony. No matter how much after-sun they slathered on, nothing could remove the stinging sensation. In vain Grace attempted to get to sleep, but there was no position that would afford her the least comfort.

For the rest of the holiday, Grace hated to admit that her mother was right, but she dutifully applied as much sun cream as she could. Each night she covered herself in after-sun, yet it did little to soothe the pain. The remaining week and a half were endured with much less enthusiasm than she had hoped. Worse still, she could see that as soon as the skin started to peel, rather than revealing nicely browned skin there was only the return of pearl-white.

On the final morning, Grace's mother helped her ensure she had packed all of her belongings in the suitcase. As her mother folded trousers and rolled T-shirts in the superhuman way mother's do to fit clothing into small spaces, Grace noticed the caramel tone to her mother's arms. It didn't make any sense to her, Grace had inherited her milky-white genes from her mother and she had been plastered in factor 50 all the time. How had she been able to develop a tan under such conditions.

"Mum, you've been holding out on me. How did your arms get so tanned?" Grace marveled, reluctantly impressed by her mother's superior skills.

"I only followed the same instructions I tried to give you," her mother replied.

"Yeah," Grace countered, "but when I was wearing sun cream nothing happened, it stopped any sun getting through."

"That's not entirely true," her mother corrected, "even factor 50 couldn't block it all out. There were some imperceptible differences. However, they weren't big enough for fast enough for you to notice. You wanted the perfect tan on day one, but our skin isn't capable of that. We can't expect to achieve all our greatest ambitions, make all the important changes, reach perfection in the blink of an eye. That would be impossible, or you would burn out like you did.

Rather, we need to let the sun convert our skin tone one ray at a time. It is only through slow and steady exposure that our skin can adapt. That way the colour lasts longer, the transformation less temporary because it has become part of us. You can't try to run faster than you are able because you just end up collapsing, which does nobody any good."

In time, Grace recovered from her brush with sun burn and went back to her pale, freckled skin. Despite that, she never forgot the realization that she had a much better chance bronzing her skin if she took it slowly rather than recklessly blasting it with sun. As long as she acknowledged the limits of her body, she could patiently work within them to affect real change.

Ethan's Mortgage

For I reckon that the sufferings of this present time are not worthy to be compared with the glory which shall be revealed in us.

- *Romans 8:18*

It was the best decision he had ever made. The garden was large enough for the children to play in without being too unwieldy. The kitchen had an island wide enough for them all to help prepare dinner around. Even the ensuite had a jacuzzi setting in the bath. On top of all that, it was down the road from the house his high school friend was also buying.

Viewing the house, making an offer and joyfully having it accepted were one thing, sitting down in the mortgage lender's beige office was quite another. The grey venetian blinds were pulled down to keep out the glare of the sun and a mug with cold coffee was still sat on the edge of the desk. There was a low buzzing of something caught in the fan and a vaguely stale smell in the air. Ethan and his wife sat across from the stranger in a shirt with rolled up sleeves and a striped tie as a badge of reliable expertise.

As he typed different variables into his computer, it suggested a limited range of options for the couple. The economic climate was relatively good with interest rates at an all time low. They could choose from an array of 2-, 5- or 10-year fixed mortgages to allow them to afford the house of their dreams. Ethan thought the 2-year fixed mortgage looked particularly attractive- they would only have to pay 1.5% interest. Even considering the size of the loan, it made for very reasonable monthly repayments. His wife Esme, however, favoured the longer-term commitment at the alarmingly higher rate of 1.9%. Ethan couldn't understand why she would want to pay more and be locked into a commitment for longer. They might be missing out on even better rates in a couple of years' time!

They took all the information home and debated the merits of each plan all night. Ethan listed all the things they could do with the extra money right now; the immediate and certain benefits. Esme, on the other hand, extolled the probable virtues of locking in a good deal now. The 0.4% wasn't much more and they could definitely afford it. For her, the future was an unknown place, which was far more likely to get worse than better than the current situation they found themselves in. Ultimately, they slept on it and Ethan conceded to her reasoning.

Over the next few months, it became apparent that Ethan's friend, John, had made the opposite choice. Whenever they went out together, he always seemed to have the extra cash to get one more round of drinks. When they looked around John's house for the first time, Ethan couldn't help but notice his friend's TV was an extra 5 inches wider. These were all little things, but it irked Ethan that he couldn't possess anything quite as nice as his friend. They were perfectly comfortable in their own place and had everything they needed, but John always seemed to be able to do just a little bit better.

One evening, as they were eating the casserole lovingly prepared by Esme on the white, ceramic plate set bought from Tesco, Ethan voiced his frustrations about being on a tighter budget than John.

"He's practically laughing in the lap of luxury," Ethan vented, as he stabbed his knife more vehemently than he intended into the innocent potato.

"We're hardly on death's door," Esme reasoned.

"Might as well be," Ethan mumbled, too quietly for his wife to hear and she had the wisdom to know this was something better left than probed.

"There isn't much difference between us," Esme reminded, "and the main thing is that we are safe and well. Things could be a lot worse."

As the two years went by in a similar manner, the outer world started to shift. 'The Economy' began to feature more heavily on every news bulletin, which was frequently being referred to as the harbinger of doom. Inflation was rising, employment was declining and everything was reportedly going in the wrong direction. Some of their friends looking to buy houses were not only astounded by the price, but were struggling to apply for a mortgage at all. As the renewal date on John's mortgage drew ever nearer, he put off approaching his mortgage broker like a sweet-tooth avoids the dentist.

When he had done so, John came around to Ethan and Esme's house with a disgruntled look on his face. As they sat in the humble surrounds of their patio garden, John chewed his burger in frustration.

"It just isn't fair!" he raged, "how do they expect me to afford over twice the amount of money I was paying before? It's not like I've just won the lottery or something."

Esme shot her husband a pointed look. Luckily, John couldn't read the 'I told you so' written across her face.

"And it's barely going to even touch the capital! Until now I was easily clearing £500 off the original debt each month, now they're barely going to let me cover the interest."

"I'm sorry to hear that mate, we'd heard things were bad, but I hadn't realized how much," Ethan commiserated, not sure what else he could say or do.

"Yeah, well neither had I," John huffed, running his hand through his hair.

"What do you think you'll do?" Ethan asked, hoping there would be a clear plan or escape route.

"I don't know," John sighed, pushing the coleslaw around his plate idly, "I could see if they want anyone to come in on Saturdays at work. The extra pay might cover it. Still, I'm going to have to cut back somewhere- go through my subscriptions I suppose and see what I can drop."

"Least you won't have to force yourself to the gym anymore," Ethan attempted to lighten the mood, hoping that for the rest of the afternoon his friend didn't turn to ask them when they're dream mortgage rate was up for renewal.

When John had gone home, Esme and Ethan stood at the sink with a pile full of dirty dishes (a dishwasher had also been deemed a luxury they could do without when there was only the two of them). Esme was washing each item and then placing it carefully in a systematic order to encourage her husband to allow them equal time to dry before coating them in the tea towel. However, Ethan appeared even more distracted than usual so was following the order below his usual poor standard.

"I wonder what I would do," he mused as he wrung the glass tumbler for the fifth time.

"What you would do when?" Esme asked, filling up the row of plates on the drying rack.

"If I were in John's shoes. I don't think I could handle

Blessings in Disguise

all those life style changes he was contemplating. I might just have to sell up and find somewhere cheaper."

"Well fortunately you don't have to worry about that," Esme reminded, taking the tumbler from her husband and putting it away in the cupboard in the hope he might pick up the next item.

"Yes, it seemed so hard and unfair before," Ethan agreed, "but now that little bit of suffering has rather paid off. 8 years of stress-free living were certainly worth the 0.5 % or whatever it was."

And although it had not seemed so at the time, Ethan had learnt that those minor disappointments imposed by a slightly higher, longer-term commitment mortgage were nothing compared to the misery he had been lucky enough to avoid.

Adam's Conducting

But now are they many members, yet but one body. [...] much more those members of the body, which seem to be more feeble, are necessary: [...] That there should be no schism in the body; but that the members should have the same care one for another. And whether one member suffer, all the members suffer with it; or one member be honoured, all the members rejoice with it.

- *2 Corinthians 12:20-26*

Adam had been asked to conduct a small orchestra for the play 'Into the Woods'. He was a good singer and pianist, but conducting was not his expertise. The task was daunting for many reasons, but Adam accepted the position and prepared for the first rehearsal as best he could.

He had worked with the actors for several months, accompanying them on the piano so that they were able to practice themselves. Week by week he became better acquainted with the music, but there was just so much of it. The play was written in two acts and three hours in length. Most companies only performed the first half, it was so long! Every song had a complex mixture of instruments and even when the actors were talking, the strings were usually plucking beneath them.

Finally, the time came for the orchestra to meet. A crew of willing musicians had been gathered together, each with different priorities and varying degrees of confidence. The violinist was so afraid of keeping up that she persuaded her friend to play with her, so that each could help one another. The violist had two different lines to share her time between, providing too much work to worry about the management of the orchestra. The flautist was exceedingly accomplished, finding most sections boringly easy. The bassoonist had played in several orchestras before, usually being paid for her time, in contrast to this group, who were all volunteers.

As is often the case, the bassoonist had many sections where he did not need to play. This gave him time to watch the rest of the orchestra to judge how well they were doing. He watched Adam with an eagle eye, aware of his own superior musical knowledge and waiting to see how this man would fare in comparison.

Blessings in Disguise

The first rehearsal did not go very well. Some of the musicians had not been able to make it, most notably the pianist, which held everything together. Everyone was new to the piece and, having never worked together before, unaccustomed to the situation. Adam in particular was struggling. He was meant to be leading the group, making it clear what everyone's role was and where they came in. However, the piece had so many changes of time that no sooner had his arm got used to one particular type of waving than it was required to do another. He tried his best, but more often than not he was following the loudest instrument, rather than deciding the pace himself.

The flautist had mumbled to herself the entire time, creating a distraction to further hinder Adam. He didn't look over to her, so she hardly thought about the effect her mutterings might have. Instead he concentrated on getting this best from the two violins, who were so engrossed in their music that they barely had time to look up from the page. When they did the pattern changed and the place was lost. However, they persevered, despite the stifled laughter from the woodwind.

When the rehearsal was finished everyone left in a group, some not even bothering to fold up their music stands so that Adam was left with even more work to do. He barely noticed as he continued practicing the most difficult sections and marking things he needed to remember on the sheet music with his trusty pencil. The flautist was unafraid to belittle their conductor as the musicians traipsed into the car park. Her views were made so plainly that the violins didn't dare contradict or offer their feelings of sympathy in case it reminded the flautist of their own ineptitude. No one would stick up for the brave effort Adam had made that evening.

The second rehearsal did not go much better. The pianist was helpful in keeping people together, but further distracted the musicians when they weren't playing. Adding the actors also worsened the situation. Here was another group of people who felt so comfortable in their own abilities that they did not perceive the importance of grafting all the elements together. Surely it would be alright on the night with no particular effort on their part. The waving of the conductor seemed to be more for his own benefit than for theirs.

They hung around in small groups, more interested in eating their sandwiches than participating. This meant that on several occasions when the wolf was meant to come in, or Cinderella was meant to be ready, no one sung. No one was even standing. The violins had to stop (having just worked out where on the page they were) and Adam had to look about himself for these performers, who were chatting in the corner. He was too quiet to shout at them, so his polite efforts to organise people took more and more time from their rehearsal. By the end, everyone was exhausted and all those not playing were lying, spread out on the floor.

To say there was discord among the members of this performance was an understatement. There was no unity at all, unless you counted solidarity on the part of key actors against the struggling strings, or the haughty woodwind holding joint contempt for the lazier singers. It was only a week before the performance and Adam was unsure whether they would even be able to survive the night. He went home, like many of the others, worried for the future and disappointed in the group.

During the ensuing week a mutiny almost broke out. The bassoonist had grown so tired of correcting Adam's conducting that he was ready to lay aside the bassoon part and conduct himself. No one would miss a single instrument if it meant the whole piece worked together better. He gained the support of the flautist immediately and the violins were too scared to show their surprise. Still, they feared having someone more judgmental glare at them whenever they made a mistake rather than Adam's encouraging smile.

However, everything changed on the final rehearsal in time for the performances. They were finally in the theatre that they were going to use, rather than an ill designed room with chairs littered about the place as obstacles. There was a distinct air of attention when Adam lifted his baton that day, every person aware of their role to play in making the musical a success.

The atmosphere was completely different. No one was worried about how good anyone else was because it was too important to get their own bit right. Adam had improved his conducting skills, but he was still far from perfect and did not always anticipate the time the actors needed. Still, his efforts did not go unnoticed and for once everyone was working together. The strings were following him, rather than each other and the bassoonist had dropped any foolish ideas of taking over. There was a peace that resided in each person's heart, a resignation to making the best of the situation.

This had a spectacular effect on the music. They were not a professional orchestra, but they were able to play with confidence. As they listened to one another, they would hear where lines were meant to come in, when melodies were meant to take over from one another and when chords were meant to change. Although there was not always complete harmony of sound, there was always a harmony of purpose and this was the greatest element in making the performance enjoyable.

Brian's Game

And let us not be weary in well doing: for in due season we shall reap, if we faint not.

- Galatians 6:9

Martin, Helen, Brian and Ann all sat down to play a game of monopoly. Helen had been uncertain, as such games usually erupted in emotional outbursts and more than one board had been flipped in the past. It seemed the competitive nature of the game brought out some of the worst, most selfish aspects of people. However, it was Christmas and Brian had dearly wanted to play.

It all started calmly enough. Ann's dog trotted off, landed on one of the brown properties, which she gladly purchased. Martin's car zoomed into the first of the light blue spaces and he snapped it up, declaring that if he threw a two next time he would be able to get another one in the set (which magically came to pass). Helen rolled a 5 and moved her thimble to the first of the stations, which she thought better to buy than leave. However, Brian moaned when he rolled a 10 and had to waste his go just visiting prison, rather than being able to advance his game plan.

This set the tone for the rest of the opening of the game. Ann did fairly well at buying a few different coloured properties for reasonable prices. Martin was able to stake claims for not only the light blue but also the yellow (obtaining all three through auctions where the other players were not interested in the places where they had landed). He was very smug to have the first, fairly expensive set and immediately put a little green house on each so that he could start charging every competitor more when they passed. Helen had landed on the opposite station and decided that contrary to the usual aim, she would try her hand at collecting all the stations.

When Martin was able to acquire the enviable purple property, Brian exclaimed, "Of course you did!" rising from the table. Ann put a steadying hand on his and Helen instinctively spread her arm to protect the board. "Fortune seems to have shined on you for no reason whatsoever, while the rest of us scrabble in the mire!"

"I can't help it if I'm just better than everyone," Martin smiled. "Besides, you could catch me any time, I barely have any money left and you still have an unbroken £500."

"That's because I've barely had the chance to buy anything- and you know it!" Brian retorted with an exasperated expression, "Your properties are twice the value of my notes and they will bring more dividends in the future, while I'll just be losing all my money to you!"

Brian's prophecy continued to come true as he landed on several yellow spaces over the next few rounds, funding Martin's purchase of several more houses. Meanwhile, Ann had managed to trade some of her cards to almost have completed both pink and green rows. Sadly, no one had landed on the remaining properties, so they were beyond her reach. Unlike Brian, she didn't see the point in complaining and just hoped she would hold onto enough money to purchase them when they eventually came up for sale.

When Helen was able to obtain her third station, she cheered and waved her hands in the air. Brian wanted to be happy for her, at least it wasn't a reason for Martin to rejoice, yet he still felt that he was in such a pitiable position himself. His strategies were thwarted on every side: whether it was Martin taking his favourite properties, Ann unwittingly removing his latest hope or just landing on the same already occupied spaces. He didn't even need to win anymore, he just wanted to feel like he could have a good go at the game.

"What's the point, I might as well just throw in the towel," Brian sighed, looking envious at Helen's minor personal victory.

"Don't say that," Helen chided, "We're still in the middle of the game: it can all work out for you. The game's not over yet," she added with a wink.

Blessings in Disguise

So they kept playing, Brian grumbling all the way. The first hint of a change was when he landed on one of the red properties. While everyone else cheered that now he would be able to collect his own set, one that no one else had even started on, Brian was still moaning about how he didn't really like this second-rate street.

Next, Ann landed on another red square and everyone let Brain have it very cheaply in an effort to keep the peace. His only comment was that he was sure to never obtain the final, crucial one. As though to defy his point, Helen managed to complete her train set, which made everyone cross their fingers not to land on any of the four squares that would cost them £200. Although it was nothing in comparison to Martin's properties, which now had 4 houses outside each of them, it made her smile to herself.

Then the fortunes altered drastically. Martin happened to land on a chance square, and beginning to believe in his own invincibility, picked it up with a hopeful grin. However, he stared dumbfounded at the words: he would be assessed for street repairs on every house he owned! Normally, such a card meant little or nothing, but having come at this time to a player so invested in houses, it was devastating. It resulted in him losing any of the ready money he had and being forced to mortgage half of his properties. This meant that he had hardly any sources of revenue left.

In that moment the spark of hope had kindled its way into Brian's heart. When Martin landed on one of his red properties, Brian kindly offered to take the nearly useless purple card off his hands instead of incurring further debt. Eager to return to the black, Martin accepted the deal. Brian put it to one side, thinking to himself that perhaps miracles were not as unlikely as they had once seemed.

Sure enough, Brian went on to land on the other purple square and acquire his first set, which everyone knew would cost them dearly as he immediately put a house on each. Both Ann and Helen happened to land on the squares that had previously been so elusive and Brian was able to fund another house on each. As one pile dwindled, another was increasing exponentially.

On the next circuit of the board, Brian obtained the last pink card Ann needed, which she happily traded with his remaining red card. Even though they both now had two sets, it was Brian who continued to bleed his opponents dry of their brightly coloured money.

By the end of the evening, Martin had been completely bankrupted. Ann was still in the game, but with only moderate sums of money. Helen, meanwhile, was out, but happy because she had achieved her aim of collecting all the stations. Brian was the indisputable winner, proudly patting his soft pillow of notes.

"There now," commented Helen, "I don't know what all that whining was about, it all worked out for you in the end."

"Yes," Brian conceded, "If only you could know the end from the beginning, you wouldn't panic so much in the middle."

Blessings in Disguise

Blessings in Disguise

ABOUT THE AUTHOR

Melissa A Regan was born in Essex in 1992. She studied English and American Literature with Creative Writing at The University of Kent, before getting her Post Graduate Degree of Education from The University of Cambridge.

Currently, she teaches at a middle school in Bedfordshire (happily a real place and not just one you get sent up the stairs to when you're supposed to be asleep!). Besides writing, she enjoys playing a variety of instruments: violin, trumpet, piano, handbells. As a devoted member of *The Church of Jesus Christ of Latter-day Saints*, Melissa's life is rich with service and purpose. Her roles within the Church, spanning from Music Chairman to leadership positions in the Young Women's and Relief Society organisations, stand as testaments to her dedication to community and spiritual growth.

In Melissa A Regan's world, writing, teaching, faith, and music converge to form a life rich in purpose and passion, with stories that resonate across ages and hearts.

Blessings in Disguise

Printed in Great Britain
by Amazon

95f7299c-4913-4ad0-bdc0-5a7894d173e4R01